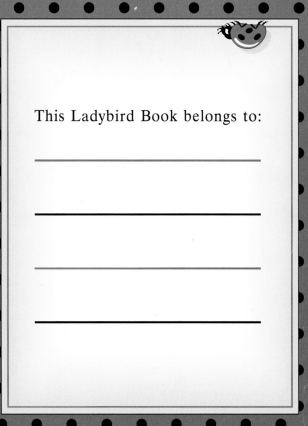

This Ladybird Book belongs to:

_____

_____

_____

_____

This Ladybird retelling
by
Audrey Daly

Ladybird books are widely available, but in case of
difficulty may be ordered by post or telephone from:

Ladybird Books – Cash Sales Department
Littlegate Road Paignton Devon TQ3 3BE
Telephone 0803 554761

A catalogue record for this book is available
from the British Library

Published by Ladybird Books Ltd Loughborough Leicestershire UK
Ladybird Books Inc Auburn Maine 04210 USA

Printed in EC

Jack and the Beanstalk

illustrated
by
MARTIN SALISBURY

based on a traditional folk tale

Once upon a time a boy named Jack lived with his mother. All they had in the world was one cow.

One day Jack's mother said, "We have no money for food. We shall have to sell the cow."

So Jack took the cow to market.
On the way, he met a man.

"If you give me your cow," said the
man, "I'll give you some magic beans
that are better than money."

Jack thought the magic beans sounded wonderful, so he gave the man the cow. Then he ran home as fast as he could.

"How much money did you get for the cow?" asked his mother.

"I got something much better than money," said Jack, showing her the magic beans.

"These beans are no good to us!" cried his mother angrily. And she threw them out of the window.

When Jack woke up the next day, his
room seemed darker than usual.
He went to the window and saw that a
huge beanstalk had grown up in the
garden overnight.

"I must find out what's at the top," he
cried, rushing outside. And he began
to climb the beanstalk.

Up and up he climbed. At last he
found himself in a bare, rocky
wilderness.

There were no plants or animals to be seen anywhere. But a long road led into the distance, and Jack began to walk along it. Towards evening he came to a castle and knocked loudly on the door.

"Could you give me some food and a bed for the night, please?" Jack asked the woman who answered.

"Oh no," said the woman. "My husband is a fierce giant who hates strangers." But Jack begged so hard that she let him in and gave him some supper.

Just as Jack was enjoying some hot soup, he heard the giant coming. The woman quickly hid Jack in a cupboard.

The giant stalked in and roared,

"Fee, fie, foe, fum,
I smell the blood of an Englishman!
Be he alive or be he dead,
I'll grind his bones to make my bread!"

"Nonsense!" said his wife. "There's no one here." And she gave the giant his supper.

When he had finished his supper, the giant bellowed, "Bring me my hen!"

His wife brought a little hen and put it on the table.

"Lay!" shouted the giant.

Jack peeped out of his hiding place.
To his amazement, every time the
giant shouted, the hen laid a little
golden egg.

When he had twelve golden eggs, the
giant fell asleep.

As soon as all was quiet, Jack crept out of the cupboard, grabbed the little hen and tiptoed out.

Then he ran and ran until he was back at the top of the beanstalk. Quickly, he climbed down and took the magic hen to his mother.

How pleased she was! "Long ago, a wicked giant stole this hen from your father," she said. "Now that we have her back, our worries are over."

Jack lived happily with his mother for a while. But he longed for adventure, and one day he decided to climb the beanstalk again.

Just as before, Jack reached the castle towards evening. And once again the giant's wife hid him when they heard the giant roar,

"Fee, fie, foe, fum,
I smell the blood of an Englishman!
Be he alive or be he dead,
I'll grind his bones to make my bread!"

After supper the giant shouted, "Fetch me my money bags!" His wife brought him some sacks filled with gold coins.

The giant emptied the sacks onto the table and counted the coins over and over again. At last he put the money back in the sacks and fell asleep.

Quick as a flash, Jack took the money and ran all the way home.

His mother was delighted when she saw the money bags. "The giant stole this money from your father," she said. "You have done well to bring it back."

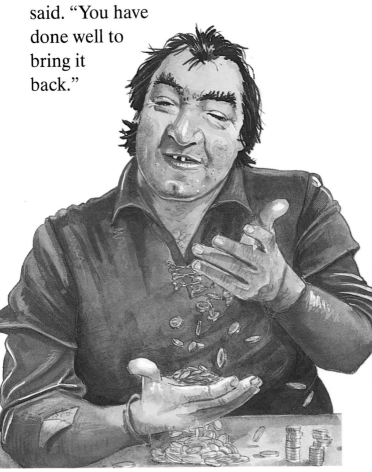

Although Jack and his mother were now rich, Jack wanted to climb the beanstalk one last time.

Everything happened just as before.

This time the giant's wife brought a beautiful golden harp. "Play!" roared the giant, and the harp began to play soft music.

The music was so gentle that it sent the giant to sleep. But when Jack crept out and seized it, the harp cried, "Master! Master!"

The giant woke up in a rage, just in
time to see Jack disappearing through
the door with the harp. "Stop, thief!"
the giant roared.

Now Jack had to run for his life.
The giant took huge strides and was
soon hard on Jack's heels. Scrambling
down the beanstalk, Jack shouted as
loudly as he could, "Mother, Mother,
bring the axe!"

When Jack's mother brought the axe,
Jack seized it with both hands and
aimed a mighty blow at the beanstalk.
Thwack! The beanstalk toppled to the
ground, and the giant tumbled down
with an earth-shaking thud.

So that was the end of the giant.
Jack and his mother were never poor
again, and they both lived happily
ever after.